This Way to the Garden

www.dk.com

LONDON • NEW YORK • STUTTGART • SYDNEY

www.dk.com

Editor   Vicci Parr
Designers   Mandy Sherliker and Ness Wood
Managing Editor   Joanna Devereux
Managing Art Editor   Chris Fraser
Production   Linda Dare
DTP Designer   Jill Bunyan
Original TV Script   Jocelyn Stevenson
Story Adaptation   Caryn Jenner
Photography   Dave King
Illustrations   Denis Ryan

First published in Great Britain in 1999 by
Dorling Kindersley Limited, 9 Henrietta Street, London WC2E 8PS

A CIP record for this book is available from the British Library.

ISBN 0-7513-6645-5

Colour reproduction by Dot Gradations Limited
Printed in Belgium by Proost

It was time for Mopatop to open his shop.
"Welcome to Mopatop's Shop," he said.
"Would you like a giant green pea? Or a
sparkly blue sea? Or a bird in a tree?"

Moosey climbed down from the attic
just as Puppyduck rushed into the shop.
"Sorry I'm late, Mopatop,"
she said. "I was planting
some things in my
garden."

"I didn't know Puppyduck had a garden,"
Moosey whispered to the bird in the tree.
"Shall I tell you what I planted in my
garden, Mopatop?" asked Puppyduck.
DING!
"Tell me later,
Puppyduck.
We've got
a customer,"
said Mopatop.

Their customer was a little mole.
"Welcome to Mopatop's Shop," said Mopatop.
"Hello there. I'm Roly Moley," said the mole.
"I'm looking for a sign."
"We have all kinds of signs," Puppyduck told
him. "Come with me. I'll show you."

Puppyduck showed Roly Moley lots of different signs.
"We have a Stop sign, and a Do Not Enter sign," she said. "And a Zebra Crossing sign."

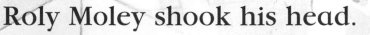

Roly Moley shook his head.

"I'm looking for a sign which says 'This Way to the Garden'."

"Hmm. I'm sure we have one of those signs here," said Puppyduck. She looked again.

"Here it is." Puppyduck held up a sign with flowers and grass, and an arrow to point the way.

"Thank you," said Roly Moley. He carried his new sign out of the shop.

"Come again!" called Mopatop.
"Now can I tell you
what I planted
in my garden?"
asked
Puppyduck.
DING!
"You'll have to
wait, Puppyduck.
We've got another
customer," said
Mopatop.

"It's me again," said Roly Moley. "I need a fence to put my sign on."
Mopatop reached onto a shelf for a white picket fence.
"How about this fence?" asked Mopatop.
"Perfect," said Roly Moley.

Roly Moley put the sign on the fence. "A nice new fence with a nice new sign showing all my friends how to get to my garden. It's absolutely lovely," he said. "Now all I need is a garden."

"What do you want in your garden, Roly Moley?" asked Mopatop.
"Let me tell you what I have in *my* garden!" said Puppyduck.

How does my garden grow?
There are teapots and pyjamas,
And rowing boats, all in a row!
There's toothpaste, and fast cars,
Saucepans and jam jars.

My garden is lovely,
No flowers at all.
Just things that are useful,
Growing healthy and tall!

Moosey and the bird laughed so hard they nearly fell over.

"I think I would like some flowers in my garden," Roly Moley told Puppyduck.

"And some grass?" suggested Mopatop.

"Oh yes!" said Roly Moley. "And could I have bees and butterflies, too?"

Mopatop laughed. "Of course."

"I've got an idea!" said Roly Moley.
"I'll pretend that I'm going to my
garden to visit me."
He strolled along towards the fence.
"Look! There's a fence with a sign
on it. 'This Way to the Garden'."
Roly Moley walked a bit further.
"And here's the garden!"
"It's a lovely garden," said Mopatop.
"Yes, it is," said Roly Moley
thoughtfully. "But something
is missing."

"Roly Moley, your garden has grass and flowers and bees and butterflies. What could be missing?" asked Mopatop.

The bird in the
tree nodded.
"Roly Moley
is right, you know.
His garden is
definitely missing
something."
"But what?"
whispered
Moosey.

"Socks!" Puppyduck
declared.
Roly Moley shook
his head.
"A teapot!" said
Puppyduck.
Roly Moley shook his
head again.
"No, it's not a teapot."

"TWEET!" The bird in the tree chirped
very loudly.
"How about me?" she asked Roly Moley.

A smile spread across Roly Moley's face. "That's it!" he said. "A bird in a tree would be perfect!"

"Of course," the bird told him. "I'm exactly what you need for your garden. And I do love gardens!"

"My garden is perfect!" said
Roly Moley.
"It certainly is," Mopatop agreed.
"But I think it could do with
some stripey pyjamas,"
said Puppyduck.
Everyone laughed.

Just then, the big clock chimed.
"It's time to close the shop," said Mopatop.
"I'll wrap up your garden for you to take
home," Puppyduck said to Roly Moley.

Puppyduck gave Roly Moley a large parcel.
"Thank you very much for the garden!"
called the little mole as he left the shop.

The next day, three invitations arrived.
Roly Moley was having a garden party.
Mopatop and Puppyduck were very excited,
and so was Moosey.